Let's Fly with Ride

Yashodhara P

Ukiyoto Publishing

All global publishing rights are held by

Ukiyoto Publishing

Published in 2023

Content Copyright © Yashodhara P

ISBN 9789359201047

*All rights reserved.
No part of this publication may be reproduced, transmitted, or stored in a retrieval system, in any form by any means, electronic, mechanical, photocopying, recording or otherwise, without the prior permission of the publisher.*

The moral rights of the author have been asserted.

This is a work of fiction. Names, characters, businesses, places, events, locales, and incidents are either the products of the author's imagination or used in a fictitious manner. Any resemblance to actual persons, living or dead, or actual events is purely coincidental.

This book is sold subject to the condition that it shall not by way of trade or otherwise, be lent, resold, hired out or otherwise circulated, without the publisher's prior consent, in any form of binding or cover other than that in which it is published.

Acknowledgement

I never planned such a story in my mind anytime. So, I know that God has inspired me to write this book "Let's fly with Ride". My writing would not be so advanced without my husband Mr. Swapan Purkayastha who meticulously reads the story and suggests me change or add a few sentences.

I'm thankful to Dr. Swati Parab for writing the foreword for the story. I requested only once, and she was very enthusiastic to write foreword for the special story "Lets Fly with Ride."

I'm always grateful to my Maa (96years) and Baba who showed me the light of Earth and always encouraged me to tread my chosen path.

Last but not the least, I am grateful to all my readers and reviewers for reading the book and critically writing the reviews.

Preface

The book "Let's fly with Ride" is a story of three sisters who have done wonders for society. This book is for those who have daughters, and they must feel proud of their daughters. Three daughters are assets of their parents especially for a father. Society, the relatives, all wanted a son in the family to keep the line of heirs, but their father knew that his daughters could touch the sky of success. He always encouraged them to fly in the sky with different coloured wings and never denied their proposals.

He knew in heart that his three daughters were special gifts from the Ultimate. So, the father kept some special names as Pine, Pony, and Ride. God always sends a person on earth for a purpose. To understand the purpose, is another blessing of God. Ride is the storyteller.

Foreword

It was an unexpected message and the most surprising thing when Dr. Jashodhara Purkayastha, my B. Ed professor, asked me to write the forward for her new book "Lets Fly with Ride". I not only learnt academic subjects from her but also values of life. It was a privilege and an honour to now be writing a foreword for a book written by one of the best professors I have ever had the good luck of being associated with.

I hope and pray that this book reaches millions of readers as surely this is one of those books that will mark its identity as one that has the power to change the mindset of society for the betterment of future women.

This book shall serve the purpose of doing just that whenever this blessed soul, Dr. Jashodhara Purkayastha, isn't in person.

Dr. Swati Parab

Director, Atharva School of Business

11th September 2023

Contents

Let's Fly With Ride!	1
Stars' Family	4
Visit Different Places.	10
Reaching Jaipur	14
A Brown Bear In The Bungalow In The Foothills	21
The First Star, Pine	26
A Leading Lady, Pony	41
Love Story Of Ride	58
How To Get Ducks In A Row	73
About the Author	*81*

Let's Fly With Ride!

A city boasting delightful year-round weather and surrounded by picturesque landscapes at the base of the lower Himalayas is teeming with exotic flora and fauna. It serves as a gateway to numerous hill stations like Mussoorie, as well as the revered towns of Rishikesh and Haridwar. This city is truly a gift from Mother Nature, with its natural wildflowers lending it a magnificent charm. The breathtaking sunrises and sunsets at the Forest Research Institute (FRI) have a blissful impact on every heart and soul.

Not only does the city possess natural beauty, but it also hosts the esteemed Doon School, established in 1935 to impart a British-style education. This prestigious institution, exclusively for boys, attracts students from all corners of the country and the world in search of a superior and more disciplined education.

The name 'Doons' is derived from the plains formed by rivers cutting through the mountains, leaving behind meandering waterways. During the monsoon season, the city is enveloped in lush greenery, with the soothing sound of streams flowing through the foothills. The overall atmosphere, environment, and ambiance of this place are nothing short of extraordinary.

Dehradun, the capital of Uttarakhand, India, is nestled at the foothills of the Himalayas. It is renowned for its pleasant climate, which prevails for most of the year. The prime season for travelers is from March to June when the weather is exceptionally agreeable. The rainy season commences in late June. Dehradun boasts a helicopter aerodrome, offering convenient access for travelers to Kedarnath and Badrinath.

Dehradun offers a multitude of captivating attractions. At the city's center, stands the six-sided Ghanta Ghor clock tower. The bustling Paltan Bazar serves as a vibrant shopping hub. Towards the southwest in Clement Town, the Mind Rolling Monastery stands as a Tibetan Buddhist center with shrine rooms inside its remarkable Great Stupa.

A prominent Dehradun attraction is the Tapkeshwar Temple, known for water cascading from the top onto the Shivalinga. This temple is located on the banks of the Tons River and has its primary shrine situated inside a substantial cave. The mythological significance of this place can be traced back to the ancient Mahabharata era when Guru Dronacharya, the royal teacher of the Pandavas and Kauravas, was believed to reside in this cave.

The Forest Research Institute is a training institute under the Indian Council of Forestry Research and Education, dedicated to natural resource services. It is a pioneering institution in the field of forestry research in India, catering to Indian Forest Service cadres and State Forest Service cadres. Notably, this location has served as the backdrop for numerous famous films due to its suitability for film shooting. The FRI is vast, so exploring its beauty thoroughly can be quite tiring in just one day.

Writing about Dehradun holds significance, as Dr. Mrs. Ride Agarwal Nirmal once worked at the Cantonment Hospital. The Cantonment General Hospital is a 14-bed facility primarily offering maternity services, with a functional labor room for normal deliveries. Dr. Ride's daily routine at the hospital became monotonous, prompting her to seek solace at the Tapkeshwar Mahadev Temple.

One day, while sitting by the clear waters of the Tons River, she reflected on how her life had changed. The refreshing breeze from the Tons River reinvigorated her and brought back old memories. In that serene setting, she began singing a devotional song in praise of Lord Shiva.

Dr. Ride, a gynecologist at the military hospital, completed her medical education at BITS Pilani, a renowned institution equipped with state-of-the-art facilities. Her academic journey, starting from her early years, was marked by excellence, and graduating from such a prestigious institution was a point of pride for any student. Subsequently, she specialized in gynecology at AIIMS. As the cool breeze from the Tons River enveloped her, Dr. Ride found herself reminiscing about the different phases of her life, each unfolding before her eyes.--

Stars' Family

Mr. Ranvir Agarwal, hailing from Jaipur, Rajasthan, was a prominent cotton businessman. His wife, Himani, was a woman of striking beauty but had discontinued her studies after completing her schooling. Himani's father, a cotton merchant himself, hailed from Udaipur, Rajasthan. Being part of a business-oriented family, discipline and punctuality were core values for them.

Jaipur, situated in the northern Indian state of Rajasthan, is renowned as one of Bharat's (India's) most affluent cities. The city boasts a robust economy driven by a thriving tourism sector, well-established infrastructure, and a diverse array of industries.

Mr. Ranvir Agarwal and Himani were blessed with three daughters, as they did not have any sons. Despite Himani's hopes for a son after their first two daughters, their third child also turned out to be a girl, leaving her feeling disheartened.

Ranvir was overjoyed to welcome another adorable baby girl into Himani's arms. He cherished his daughters immensely and gave them unique names without particular meanings. The eldest daughter was named Pine, followed by Pony and Ride. All three daughters were exceptionally beautiful and excelled in various fields. Pine became a chartered accountant, Pony pursued a career in architecture, and Ride became a doctor. Not only were they academically gifted, but they also displayed remarkable athletic abilities. The eldest was a top-tier badminton player, Pony excelled in horse riding and participated in annual Polo events, and Ride was a state-level chess player.

Mr. Ranvir held a deep belief that his three daughters would carry forward the family's name and legacy. He had this conviction from the very beginning, even when they were just starting school. He firmly believed in the saying, 'Morning shows the day,' and thus, he never refused any of their aspirations. He wholeheartedly encouraged them to pursue their passions, as he had complete trust in their ability to maintain the family's reputation intact.

During their honeymoon in Shillong, Meghalaya, Bharat, Mr. Ranvir and Himani decided to name their child Pine after the abundant pine trees they encountered. This marked Himani's first visit to a hill station, where she was captivated by the rows of majestic pine trees.

Shillong was chosen as their honeymoon destination on the recommendation of Ranvir's friend, Dr. Shan. Dr. Shan had spent his childhood in Shillong when his father, Lieutenant Mr. Pradeep Batra, was stationed there. He often referred to Shillong as the "Scotland of the East" and encouraged Mr. Ranvir to experience its beauty.

Dr. Shan strongly insisted that Ranvir visit Shillong, despite Ranvir's lack of prior experience with hill stations. Ranvir expressed concerns about the distance from his hometown of Jaipur, but Dr. Shan assured him that the journey would be worth it, highlighting the favorable climate, picturesque scenery, and more. Shillong, the capital of Meghalaya, is located in the northeast and is well-connected by both flights and trains to Guwahati, the capital of Assam (Dispur).

Before their marriage, Dr. Shan assisted Ranvir in booking a flight to Guwahati and recommended hiring a cab from the airport to Shillong. He also advised Ranvir to pack warm clothing and even helped him secure a hotel reservation in Shillong.

Ranvir and Himani embarked on a two-day journey to Shillong in the month of June. They explored Lady Hydri Park and Ward Lake, and during their visit to the latter, they encountered a small zoo, the highlight of which was a bear. They discovered that this park was aptly named the Manicure Gardens. Ward Lake, surrounded by walking trails, caught Himani's interest as she observed the variety of fish in the lake, lured by offerings of groundnuts and peas from visitors. They also relished a boat ride on the lake.

Their exploration continued with a visit to the Don Bosco Centre for Cultural Features, followed by the exploration of two grand churches nearby. The following day, they ventured to Golf Link, another of Shillong's attractions. Himani was captivated by the natural beauty of Shillong and declared it the ideal honeymoon destination. At Golf Link, they marveled at the Pine tree zone, feeling truly enchanted. Overwhelmed by the beauty of the Pine trees surrounding them, Ranvir playfully suggested, "Let's name our first child Pine." They both laughed heartily, and their joyous laughter echoed through the area, harmonizing with the breeze rustling through the Pine trees and the chirping of birds.

Shillong Pine is one of Bharat's most renowned varieties of pinewood. Shillong Golf Link stands as the largest and most natural in the country.

Shillong is celebrated for its enchanting waterfalls and lush forests. As the capital of Meghalaya, it is one of Bharat's most pristine and picturesque hill stations, graced with a lush blanket of beautiful Pine trees encircling the city and its surroundings.

Golf Link, spanning an area of 5873 yards and featuring a par of 70, challenges golfers with its tight fairways. The course at the Shillong Golf Club is covered in indigenous local grass that has a firming effect on the soil, adding to the challenge for players (Source: Google). During their visit, they also explored Cherrapunji.

After two days of exploration, they returned home, far from their native Rajasthan. Himani, brimming with happiness, enthusiastically shared the beauty of Shillong with everyone, encouraging them to experience it for themselves. Despite her limited formal education, Himani composed a poem about Shillong. She felt somewhat shy about showing it to her husband. However, when Ranvir read the poem, he lovingly embraced his wife and said, "You have a talent for composing poems. In your spare time, you should write more. I'll get you a diary today."

Shillong

I did not know the name of Shillong,

It sounds pitter patter of tiny feet,

I was repeating the light knocking sounds,

With happiness and cheerfulness in my mind.

Saw the grove of pine encircling the place!

Milk like water meandering from the hill,

Felt like running and drink with a thrill,

Asking all members to visit with grace.

The story behind the names of their children, especially their firstborn, Pine, is intriguing. Two years into their marriage, they were blessed with a baby girl, and they chose to name her Pine.

Two years later, another daughter was born, and Mr. Agarwal named her Pony, a decision that raised concerns among family members who worried that she might face teasing in school. However, when Pony started walking at the tender age of ten months, it became evident that she might have a promising future as a runner.

At the age of ten months, Himani, their mother, became pregnant again, this time with the expectation of delivering a baby boy. In October, she gave birth to yet another beautiful baby girl, much to the chagrin of family members, especially Ranvir's mother, who were concerned about the lack of a male heir in the family. Nevertheless, Mr. Ranvir reassured his mother, saying, "I'll name her Ride. It signifies being carried or moving with great momentum. She will always lead us on an exciting journey." Ranvir made a mental note of this decision.

> *"Trip is important and obligation in life,*
> *To know the value of file under the pile.*

Visit Different Places.

Every year, the Agarwal family embarked on various trips, joined by their three daughters and grandparents. During one such expedition, they decided to explore the foothills of the Himalayas. Their enchantment with the place led them to extend their stay, driven by their daughters' deep affection for the location. The three girls wholeheartedly implored Mr. Agarwal to contemplate the idea of purchasing a house in the area, a wish he never hesitated to fulfill. However, Mrs. Himani Agarwal, his wife, was less enthusiastic about the idea of acquiring a house in this remote location and openly expressed her reservations, a sentiment shared by Mr. Agarwal's parents.

Nonetheless, Mr. Ranvir Agarwal began to explore the area and enlisted the assistance of a real estate agent named Mr. Virinchi. After inspecting multiple properties, they stumbled upon a spacious two-story building nestled close to the hill. The house featured a generous downstairs corridor. In the evening, Mr. Agarwal, accompanied by his three daughters, revisited the property and found themselves quite enamored with it. As they surveyed the maize garden flanking both sides of the house, the youngest daughter, Ride, enthusiastically exclaimed, "Oh no! I was really taken with the maize garden. I was actually going to suggest,

Daddy, that we cultivate some maize here. We could also plant apple trees, and every summer, we could return to this place."

Pony suggested, "If someone wishes to visit this place, we can even consider renting the house. We could place advertisements in newspapers and have Mr. Virinchi assist our guests. What do you think, Daddy?"

Daddy responded, "We can certainly mull over that proposal later. For now, our priority is to have a conversation with the house's owner."

Mr. Virinchi then introduced them to the owner, Mr. Prasad Nirmal, a ninety-year-old man who resided in a small house within a bustling area near the market. He lived alone and expressed his wish to sell the house due to his inability to maintain it any longer. Mr. Nirmal explained that he had lived there with his family a few years ago, but his eyesight had deteriorated to the point where he could hardly discern anyone walking in the vicinity at night.

During their discussion, Mr. Agarwal inquired about Mr. Nirmal's banking arrangements. As they conversed, Mr. Agarwal discovered that Mr. Nirmal had served as an army officer in the Indian Army. After gathering all the necessary details, Mr. Agarwal requested that the full payment be made into a bank account, with only ten thousand rupees in cash.

This momentous transaction unfolded in the presence of Mr. Agarwal's three daughters: Pine, Pony, and Ride. Their joy radiated as they warmly embraced and kissed their father, conveying their delight with his decision. Mr. Agarwal then explained to Mr. Prasad ji, "I made this deal for the sake of my three daughters. Everything I do, I do for them. Each year, we embark on journeys far and wide, and if they desire something, I promptly make it happen. This time, all three fell in love with this place and wish to visit it frequently. Even though they are my daughters, I've raised them without distinction from boys. I see no difference between sons and daughters; to me, all three are both my sons and daughters. Thus, I am wholeheartedly committed to providing them with everything they desire.

The house they acquired was an expansive bungalow, a two-story structure positioned a short distance from the mountains. Despite its slight separation, the scenic view from the house left one at a loss for words. The small pine trees were meticulously arranged in a sequential pattern, forming an almost artistic design. The sunrise, framed by the pine trees, cast a soothing red hue, presenting a spectacular sight.

Adjacent to the bungalow was a maize garden that filled the family with delight upon their initial glimpse. The bungalow featured numerous rooms, divided into two parts by a generous corridor. The grandfather speculated, "I believe the bungalow's owner must have considered two sons when designing it, ensuring that each could have one portion.

During their initial two-day stay, they refrained from residing in the bungalow due to its lack of cleanliness. However, after finalizing the deal, they returned with the necessary paperwork. Mr. Ranvir expressed his gratitude to Mr. Prasadji, saying, "You are welcome to visit and stay at the house anytime. We may have purchased it, but you were the one who nurtured this house from its early days, from a foundation of pebbles to a solid boulder. This must have been your dream house in your younger days, and you successfully kept your family together despite your transferable job."

Mr. Prasadji thanked Mr. Ranvir. On their way back from Prasadji's house, they acquired a new lock and key from the market, ensuring the house was securely locked. Mr. Ranvir instructed Virinchi to diligently care for the house and offered him a fixed salary for the task. He also conveyed to Virinchi, "Please ensure the house is cleaned at least twice a week, and handle any necessary repairs." Virinchi nodded in agreement, and with that, Mr. Ranvir handed over the keys to Virinchi before departing after two days.

Reaching Jaipur

Upon returning to Jaipur, the three daughters were eager to visit Kasol, a quaint village in Himachal Pradesh, Bharat, and undertake the task of renovating the bungalow for potential rentals. Sitting down with their father, they candidly expressed their interest, saying, "We would like to renovate the house in Kasol and offer it for rent. We were thinking of heading there within a few days." Mr. Agarwal, ever supportive of his daughters' aspirations, immediately reached out to Mr. Virinchi.

The plan was set in motion. In May, Ride, enjoying a month-long vacation, had the freedom to embark on this project. Pine, as a chartered accountant, approached her boss to request some work that could be managed remotely for seven days. Pony, an architect, contacted her friend Ajay to collaborate on planning the Kasol trip. Ajay, intrigued by the idea, inquired, "Kasol! Why?" To which Pony replied, "I'll provide you with all the details, but please arrange for some work to be done from home for seven days."

Within a mere fifteen days, all arrangements were made, and the three sisters, joined by two friends, Ria Munshi (Ride's friend) and Ajay Baghel (Pony's friend), set off for Kasol to bring their renovation plans to life.

Ajay hailed from a royal Rajput family known for their hotel business across Rajasthan and various other locations in India. Pony and Ajay had been close friends since their college days, having both studied at JJ College of Architecture in Mumbai, Bharat. They were both top-ranking students at the University of Mumbai, spending four years together in the bustling city. During this period, Pony resided in a girl's hostel near her college, while Ajay lived in a hostel in Bandra, Mumbai.

Ria had been Ride's classmate since their school days, and they both had the opportunity to study medicine at BITS Pilani. The two families were closely connected.

Upon their arrival in Kasol, the group decided to stay in their recently acquired bungalow. Mr. Ranvir had arranged for Mr. Virinchi to ensure the house was cleaned before their arrival. The following day, Virinchi introduced them to a handyman named Kutti, tasked with painting and repairing the house. Pine, being the eldest among them, directed Kutti to commence the work promptly.

In the evening, after their meal, Ajay proposed sharing a ghost story. He began, "It's not just a story; it's a true incident. Ghost stories!" Intrigued, everyone drew closer.

Ajay launched into his story, saying, "Back in our first year, all the seniors would assign us their projects, and we'd toil away at them through sleepless nights. Sometimes, we'd be so sleep-deprived that we'd arrive late for college. One day, the four of us decided to visit the Elephanta Caves. These caves house an impressive collection of cave temples dedicated to Lord Shiva. They are located on Elephanta Island, or Gharapuri, in Mumbai Harbour, about 10 kilometers east of Mumbai, Bharat. The visiting hours for Elephanta Caves are from 09:30 am to 05:30 pm, with the first ferry departing from the Gateway of India jetty at 09:00 am, taking approximately an hour to reach Elephanta Island.

We boarded the ferry at 10 in the morning and arrived at around 11. Since all four of us were new to Mumbai, we were excited about the trip. None of us had seen the Arabian Sea before, so we savored the ferry ride, with the cool sea breeze rejuvenating our minds.

The caves themselves house ancient Buddhist and Hindu cave temples that are over 2000 years old. The Hindu temples are adorned with stone sculptures representing the Hindu Saiva cult. Exploring the Elephanta Caves is like embarking on a treasure hunt through ancient caves and sculptures. The dark tunnels and hidden carvings give you a sense of being on a real-life adventure. The grand statues of gods and goddesses are truly impressive. The ferry ride was thrilling and the exploration within the caves equally so. A visit to the Elephanta Caves is a must for all visitors.

Pine interjected, saying, "We visited Elephanta when Pony was in Mumbai. Please go ahead with the story." Ajay responded, "I was preparing all of you by talking about the Elephanta Caves, so listen to the story attentively. No one should be frightened."

Ria inquired, "Is it very scary?" To which Ajay replied, "I can't say if it's scary, but it's certainly unbelievable." He then continued with the narrative, "After returning from Elephanta, we were all very tired. The four of us planned to have dinner at Churchgate station and then head back to our hostel with the intention of sleeping soundly upon arrival. We had dinner, and it was around eleven at night when we boarded the local train and made our way to our hostel room.

Upon entering our room, a fellow student named Pankaj rushed in and delivered the shocking news that Piyush had been found dead in his room. All three of us began calling out for Piyush. I couldn't believe the news, thinking, 'Where is Piyush now? He was with us the entire day. We went to Elephanta together.' It was only then that I realized Piyush hadn't interacted much with us that day." The two friends who accompanied Ajay remained silent and unable to utter a word.

Ajay then asked Pankaj, "What time did you receive this message?"

Pankaj responded, "Around 10 in the morning when you left the hostel." Ajay questioned, "Are you certain it was 10? We boarded the ferry at 10. Piyush was with us all day, even when we returned to the hostel."

As the story unfolded, fear gripped the group, and Pine asked Ajay, "I can't believe it. You must be joking. He was with you the entire day. He sat on the ferry, visited

Elephant Caves, and returned with you." Ajay explained, "After receiving the news, we were all terrified. We stayed up all night discussing why Piyush had been so quiet that day. He even left the table for a while during our meal. But one question has always haunted me: how did he accompany us back to the hostel? The three of us left the Bandra hostel after the incident. To this day, when I think back to my college days, this incident still haunts me. I often wonder, isn't this incident beyond the realm of science?"

The narrative left everyone deeply unsettled. It wasn't a ghost story but a tragic incident. None of them could sleep that night. Pine urged everyone to rest properly, as Kutti would arrive to commence painting and other work at 9 in the morning.

In the morning, Virinchi organized breakfast for everyone. At 9, Kutti arrived with a team of workers and requested that they all go for a walk.

Ria and Ride strolled toward the market. On their way back, Ride noticed a man walking in front of them. He was tall, fair, and well-built, moving with an air of confidence. Ride remarked to Ria, "Look at the man up ahead. He doesn't seem to be from around here. He must be a visitor from another city."

The man turned and offered a warm smile as he responded, "I'm actually from this place. My grandfather resides here, and I come to visit him often. We have a large bungalow near the mountain, but no one has been looking after it. It's a bit challenging for my grandfather to manage such a big property at his age, as he's now ninety years old."

Ride, her voice soft and curious, inquired, "What is your grandfather's name, and what should we call you?"

The man replied, "My grandfather is Prasad Nirmal, and I'm Paramjeet Nirmal. I'm currently posted in Shimla, so I can visit this place frequently."

Ride was excited by the answer and exclaimed, "We've recently purchased the house from Prasadji, and it's wonderful to meet his grandson here in the market." She continued, "Let's find a place to sit and introduce ourselves." They settled at a nearby tea stall, where Ride explained, "Fifteen days ago, we came here as a family. We fell in love with this place and decided to buy a bungalow here. Fortunately, we found this house, and our father purchased it from Prasad uncle. I'm Ride, and this is my best friend, Ria. My two sisters, Pine and Pony, along with our brother Ajay, are exploring the other side of the market. We're back here now to renovate the house."

Paramjeet listened attentively, his head slightly bowed, and he expressed, "I'm feeling a bit disheartened. As the heir to the family, I couldn't manage my grandfather's property. I'm always occupied with my job and interior work, so I never thought about this property. I'm glad that this property has fallen into the right hands. I hope you all will take good care of it, and my grandpa can continue to live here peacefully."

Ride thanked Paramjeet and said, "I hope we'll meet again soon. Since your grandfather is here, and our house was once yours, we are bound to cross paths. I'm not sure if I'll extend my stay here or not." Paramjeet bid them farewell and departed.

A Brown Bear In The Bungalow In The Foothills

Kasol is a charming hamlet nestled in Himachal Pradesh's Kullu district, Bharat. It's perched in the serene Parvati Valley, along the banks of the Parvati River, lying between Bhuntar and Manikaran. Kasol is approximately 30 kilometers away from Bhuntar and 36 kilometers from Kullu town.

Ajay, our brother, ventured into the local market to interact with tourists visiting Kasol. He learned from a hotelier that exploring nearby areas like Kheer Ganga or the dense Kasol forests comes with some risk. Brown bears are known to roam the dense deodar forests of the Parvati Valley, often encountered in the mountainous terrain of Kasol. Ajay shared that he had seen videos featuring these brown bears in the Parvati Valley.

In general, the brown bear is among the most widely distributed bear species globally, with significant populations found in many parts of Eurasia and North America.

Foothills, also known as piedmont, are geographical regions characterized by gradual increases in elevation at the base of mountain ranges or higher hill ranges. They serve as a transitional zone between low-lying plains and areas with more pronounced topographical features like mountains, hills, and uplands.

Around 2:00 in the afternoon, the five of them returned to the house after their day's activities. Virinchi, their trusted uncle, had a meal ready for them. The house workers had accomplished something remarkable within just three to four hours – they'd successfully completed painting the rooms, transforming the space.

As they settled into the house, Virinchi offered a word of caution. He advised them not to venture outside after dark, explaining that one of the latches was not very secure, and it would be replaced the following day. His concern for their safety was evident.

At around 10:00 at night, the surrounding area grew eerily quiet, cloaked in darkness. Suddenly, they were startled by a continuous rattling noise, as if hard objects were colliding in the nearby maize garden. They soon realized that the corn in the garden was not yet fully grown; it was baby corn. Curiosity compelled them to peer through a window, so they dimmed the lights in their room.

Their gazes met a surprising sight – a large brown bear was near the garden. They couldn't help but be petrified; they had never been face to face with such a massive bear before. Fear washed over them, and they shivered. Their dread only escalated when they heard an unusual sound coming from the corridor. Their hearts pounded as they rushed to the closed door, catching sight of the formidable bear.

The bear's shaggy fur appeared to ripple rhythmically as it moved. Ria screamed in fright, but Pine quickly muffled her cries, realizing that the bear's agitation could bring them even more trouble. The scene was undeniably terrifying but also strangely captivating, almost like a movie scene.

The bear proceeded down the corridor, leaving the five of them breathless as they waited near the door for about half an hour. Strangely, there was no sign of the bear in the corridor when they looked again. The fear of the encounter left them unable to turn on the lights or sleep soundly that night. As dawn broke, they managed to get a brief two hours of sleep before being awakened by a loud noise – it was Virinchi urgently calling them.

Virinchi inquired, "How was the door in the front corridor accessible? I was genuinely surprised when I saw it. There were no latches, nothing. I became quite alarmed and tried to contact you by calling and banging on the door with urgency."

The group was eager to discuss the bear encounter from the previous night, but Pine hushed them all, taking the opportunity to explain how the brown bear had entered the corridor.

Upon hearing the details, Virinchi instructed Kutti to install additional latches right away, emphasizing the importance of top-quality latches for their safety.

When morning came, they rushed to inspect the maize garden. They discovered that the maize plants were in complete disarray. However, their relief was evident when they reached the other side of the garden and found the corn garden had been left undisturbed. Kutti informed them that bears had a particular fondness for corn.

During their visit, a boy approached and informed Kutti that some villagers had spotted a bear slowly crossing the road. Late at night, a few people in the market had even witnessed the brown bear walking at a leisurely pace.

Ride chimed in, saying, "We're both delighted and thrilled that we encountered a massive bear so close."

The sentiment was shared by everyone, with Ria expressing her only regret: "The unfortunate part is that we didn't manage to capture a video of the brown bear. It was right there, and we were so near, but fear and fascination took precedence over the thought of filming."

Ajay, standing at a distance, had a mischievous smile on his face and admitted, "I actually have a video."

His revelation piqued the group's interest. Ride exclaimed, "A video! That's fantastic, Ajay Bhaiya! How were you so composed that you managed to capture a video during such a frightening moment? We were trembling with fear, and you were filming? Incredible! Please, you must show us the video."

Ajay, being wise, responded, "Not now. The memory of the incident and the image of that massive brown bear are still vivid in our minds. I want this memory to remain as fresh as possible. The actual experience and watching a video are two distinct things. After several years, when the vividness of the moment has faded, the video will serve as a time capsule. Don't you think?"

Pony, who had been close friends with Ajay for a long time, concurred, "I completely agree with Ajay. Regardless of how often we recall this event, life's busy schedule can sometimes dull our memories. This video will offer us a fresh perspective on that unforgettable day."

After discussing it with the others, Ajay proposed, "I'll upload the video once we return to Jaipur. It will provide a unique viewpoint for future visitors as they explore this area. We're thinking of transforming this bungalow into a hotel and arranging for guided tours. Perhaps we'll even have a small car for sightseeing."

The idea found favor with everyone, and they were all in agreement.

The First Star, Pine

Pine, at 26 years old, possessed a tall, slim, and fair appearance. Her long, flowing hair was a remarkable feature, enhancing her overall beauty. She looked stunning in a variety of outfits, with sarees adding a mature touch to her appearance. She had a particular fondness for chiffon sarees. One day, after returning a bit early from her firm, her mother, Himani, suggested they go to the nearby mall. Pine adorned herself in a pink chiffon saree with black spots, paired with matching pink earrings and a small black pendant. Her mother, being her obedient daughter from childhood, was an affectionate presence within their family.

Together, they ventured to the mall. While at the mall, Himani decided to browse through the selection of ornaments at Shopper's Stop. Pine suggested, "If you're looking to buy ornaments, Mom, I'd recommend visiting the nearby Tanishq store beside the mall. Why not get the ornaments there today?"

In response to Pine's suggestion, her mother replied, "We'll do some shopping here, have a meal at the café on the fourth floor, and then head to Tanishq."

After purchasing a variety of dresses and other items, they made their way to the fourth-floor café. While placing their order, Pine noticed her mother suddenly embrace a lady. Pine observed the scene from a distance and ordered pizza, her mother's preference, and two cappuccinos. As she returned to the table with the order, her mother's friend asked, "Is this your daughter?"

Himani proudly introduced Pine, saying, "Yes, she's Pine, my eldest daughter. She's a Chartered Accountant at a prestigious firm. Today, she left the office early, and I asked her to join me here. Pine, this is my school friend, Rita. It's been at least ten years since we last met, and it's quite a sudden reunion today."

Rita expressed, "I've come here for some shopping. My son, Akash, asked me to come along. He's visiting a close friend who lives nearby. So, he suggested I wait here at the cafeteria. Himani, your daughter is not only beautiful but also highly educated."

Pine felt slightly embarrassed and offered, "Masi (Aunty), I've ordered my mom's favorite pizza. Would you like me to order the same for you? And a cappuccino, too."

Before Rita could respond, a young man in his late twenties spoke up from behind, saying, "Mom, I'm here. I'll order your favorite burger and garlic bread. I know you enjoy having cold drinks with these items." He proceeded to place their snack order.

Rita then introduced her son Akash, sharing, "He's also a Chartered Accountant and is working in a prestigious firm in Mumbai. He resides in Bandra, Mumbai, Bharat. After completing his studies, he initially worked in Rajasthan but changed jobs within two years and now he's in Mumbai. I also have a daughter, Manali, who's married and living in Singapore. Her husband is an engineer. Manali, too, is an engineer and an alumnus of IIT Kanpur. But I've been talking endlessly. Now, please tell me more about your family, Himani."

Himani, gesturing towards Pine, began, "This is my eldest daughter, Pine Agarwal. There's an interesting story behind her name, which I'll share with you when we meet next time. My second daughter is Pony Agarwal, an architect who works in an architectural firm. The youngest one is Ride, who is in her final year of medicine and studying at BITS Pilani. My husband, Mr. Ranvir, is a cloth merchant and has a textile factory near Jaipur. We also have my in-laws at home; both of them are quite elderly. I hope this time you'll remember my family's history."

While they were dining, Pine and Akash shared a warm and silent connection, exchanging sweet smiles throughout the meal. After they had finished their food, they left the mall, and both Himani and Rita exchanged phone numbers.

Two days later, Rita called Himani and asked, "Would it be acceptable if our family paid you a visit today?"

Himani responded enthusiastically, "Of course! You and your family are welcome to come. If you're planning to arrive in the evening, please join us for dinner as well."

Mr. Ranvir's father, Mr. Rohit Agarwal, had also been a cloth merchant in his time. The textile mill was established during Ranvir's era, as he was a diligent and intelligent individual.

The next evening, which was a Saturday, Rita arrived at the Agarwal residence with her family. She introduced her husband, Mr. Ankur Gupta, and their only son, Akash. Their daughter was currently in Singapore. Rita mentioned that her mother-in-law wasn't feeling well that day, or she would have been present to meet everyone. Rita then turned to Himani and requested introductions to the rest of the family.

Himani obliged, saying, "This is my father-in-law, Mr. Rajiv Agarwal, and my mother-in-law, Seema Agarwal, whom I affectionately call Amma. You met Pine that day; she's Pony, my second daughter, and here's my youngest daughter, Ride. Please have some snacks and tea now. We will have dinner after 7:00."

"We have come here with a special reason," began Mr. Ankur Gupta. "My son, Akash, and my wife, Rita, have taken a liking to your daughter, Pine. If everyone is in agreement, particularly Pine, we would like to propose a family relationship."

Himani's family was taken aback by this unexpected proposal. While they had been searching for a suitable match for Pine, they hadn't anticipated such a promising one coming along so soon. Himani called Pine over to sit with them. Pine was dressed in a pistachio green outfit that day. Rita asked the family members to create a space for Akash and Pine to converse freely.

Pine escorted Akash to the terrace of the house. There, Akash asked Pine, "On the first day we met, I spoke to my mother about my choice. We work in the same field, and I believe that will help us understand each other better. How do you feel about this?"

Pine replied, "I hadn't contemplated such possibilities, but I trust my parents' judgment. If they agree, I am open to it."

Akash added, "Oh, I forgot to mention one thing; my one condition is that after we get married, you'll need to come to Mumbai immediately and find a job there."

Pine responded, "That might not be possible. I can inquire about a transfer to Mumbai from my current job. We have a good relationship with everyone, but it seems you are becoming quite demanding from now on."

Akash clarified, "No, I don't mean to be demanding. You can ask my family members whether I'm demanding or not. But if you agree, I don't want to spend a single day without you."

After they descended from the terrace, Akash's mother asked Pine, "Is everything going well?"

Pine replied, "Yes, aunty. I have faith in my parents and grandparents. I believe they will choose what's best for me."

Hearing Pine's response, Rita was deeply impressed and thought to herself that today's generation still held great respect for their parents and family.

After two months, the wedding was arranged. They say that "marriage is made in heaven." Marriage has been a joyous institution across generations and will endure until the end of time.

In the olden days, a wife's role was primarily to care for the family, give birth to children, nurture them, and often set aside her own wishes. In today's world, women have more opportunities to pursue their aspirations. They have the freedom to choose their life partners. In a progressive society, every individual, regardless of gender, has the right to select their spouse. While traditions like horoscope matching and numerology are still observed, Akash's and Pine's horoscopes were a perfect match.

During their two months of phone conversations, Pine often told Akash, "Marriage differs from married life. In married life, love and adaptability go hand in hand. In my opinion, a successful marriage comes from both partners molding themselves and harmonizing with the circumstances.

Akash responded, "Marriage and love must go hand in hand. If we aim to live together harmoniously for years, we must truly understand each other. Love and trust are the foundation of a successful marriage. To love one another means to be united, as if two bodies share one soul within the institution of marriage. A fulfilling sex life is also an essential aspect of a married relationship. When differences in opinion arise, it's crucial to engage in respectful discussions. In a happy marriage, the key lies in respecting each other's perspectives and taking care of each other's well-being. Offering praise and compliments from time to time holds great significance. While love is essential for a lasting marriage, managing anger and frustration is equally important."

After two months, Akash and Pine united in matrimony. The Pandit explained the principles of marriage to the couple.

Panditji elaborated, "Saptapadi, also known as Mangal Pheras, involves walking around the sacred fire. The Saat Pheres, or seven vows, bind the bride and groom as husband and wife, with each vow holding deep significance. The Saat Pheres, a pivotal component of a Hindu wedding, require the bride and groom to encircle the holy fire together. The couple initiates the fire, channeling their prayers through the fire to various Hindu deities for a prosperous future. Each vow is read aloud by the priest before the couple is declared husband and wife.

The first vow in Hindu marriage is a prayer for food and nourishment. We beseech God to provide us with nourishing sustenance, enabling us to live a contented life filled with respect."

The second vow entails seeking physical, mental, and spiritual strength to navigate life together. During the third round, the groom pledges to work tirelessly, putting forth his utmost efforts to ensure the prosperity of their home and the education of their children.

The bride, in turn, vows to diligently manage their resources and dedicate her love wholeheartedly to her husband, with all other men in her life taking a secondary place. She promises unwavering loyalty, maintaining her purity and faithfulness, especially to her husband.

In the fourth vow, the groom expresses gratitude to the bride for making his life beautiful and whole through this sacred union. He vows to respect both families and honor her wishes. She will be a part of all his significant decisions, and he will value her opinions.

The bride, on the other hand, promises to stand by her husband in all family, ritual, and religious matters, supporting his decisions. She will respect his choices and consider his perspective in her own decisions. In times of adversity, she will shield him and be prepared to make the ultimate sacrifice for his sake.

In the fifth vow, the couple commits to standing by each other through life's joys and sorrows, showing deep understanding and care. They seek divine blessings for healthy children and pledge to nurture them with strong values and provide a prosperous upbringing.

The sixth vow is a pledge to love and respect each other and to stand united in times of both happiness and sorrow. They jointly seek divine blessings for a long, joyful, and prosperous life to fulfill their duties and responsibilities towards each other.

The seventh and final vow solidifies their commitment as husband and wife, uniting their souls and binding them together with a divine thread of togetherness. They promise to love and support each other for all eternity, walking the path of life as devoted companions, sharing everything and cherishing one another unconditionally. They vow to uphold the sanctity of all seven vows with pure and honest intentions.

Akash tied the mangal sutra and applied sindoor in Pine's parting, and the priest declared them as husband and wife. Following the seven pheras, Akash and Pine received blessings from their elders.

The wedding was attended by numerous guests, including relatives who bestowed their blessings upon the newly married couple. The morning after the wedding, with tearful eyes, the bride and groom departed from the bride's parents' home.

Prior to their marriage, Pine had informed Akash, "We will go on our honeymoon to our bungalow in Kasol.

They spent their two-day honeymoon in Kasol and Manikaran, Himachal Pradesh. Fortunately, during this visit, they didn't encounter any bears in the bungalow, but Akash was still eager to see the brown bear, so he watched their video on YouTube. Manikaran is a picturesque place with a Gurdwara situated beside the flowing Parvati River. During their time in Manikaran, they explored the hot springs, visited the Gurdwara, and savored langar there.

After their honeymoon and pagphere ceremony, they departed for Mumbai. Mumbai was relatively new to Pine, as she had only visited once when her sister Pony was studying there. Akash's flat was located in Bandstand, Bandra.

Bandra Bandstand is a long promenade along the western coastline of Mumbai. It serves as a popular jogging track and park, offering breathtaking views of the sea. People often gather there to witness the long, crashing waves that reach the road's barricades. The area also boasts additional attractions, including Bandra Fort and Mount Mary Church. Hotel Sea Rock was once a luxurious restaurant in Bandstand, Bandra, but it was destroyed in the 1993 bomb blast.

One day, they visited a racecourse near Mahalaxmi station, which has an oval-shaped layout. While watching the horse race, Pine reminisced about an incident when her sister Pony had a fall while practicing polo. Their father rushed to her side, cradled her in his arms, and brought her to the first aid room. He reassured Pony, emphasizing that such setbacks are part of the learning process and the journey towards success. He instilled in them the importance of resilience and perseverance, serving as their unwavering source of support.

From her balcony, Pine enjoyed the breathtaking panoramic view of the Arabian Sea. Coming from Jaipur, which was a relatively dry place, she had never witnessed such a wide expanse of the sea before. Pine had heard about the revolving restaurant, but Akash informed her, "There is no revolving restaurant anymore. With the new construction of buildings, you can enjoy stunning views throughout Mumbai. There's a well-known market, Elco Market, here in Bandstand. You can find everything from branded clothes to more affordable options. We can visit it one evening." Pine was thrilled to discover the convenience of their surroundings. Mount Mary Church hosted a fair every year on the 8th of September.

In no time, both of them resumed their respective jobs, which were conveniently located not far from their flat. In the mornings, after breakfast, they headed to work. Their office had a good canteen offering subsidized prices. In the evenings, Pine and Akash would prepare their home-cooked meals together. Their daily routines were running smoothly. After two years, they welcomed a baby girl into their family. Pine's mother, Himani, and Akash's mother, Rita, came to help look after the baby. When the baby reached three months, Rita returned to Jaipur, leaving Himani to stay for an additional two months. Pine began utilizing the office day care to care for her baby, Jasmin. She would go to the attached day care center during work hours to breastfeed her daughter. When Jasmine turned two, they devised a new plan. Both of them decided to leave their jobs and start their own business in Jaipur.

After finalizing their plan, they informed their parents. Pine's father, Mr. Ranvir, readily agreed to the proposal, always being supportive of his daughter's wishes. He promptly called Pine, saying, "I'm thrilled with the proposal. I know Mr. Patel; he offers office premises for rent. I'll ask him to show me suitable locations. Once you arrive, you can decide on the ideal location. When are you planning to leave Mumbai?"

In contrast, Aakash's father, Mr. Ankur Gupta, was generally a pessimistic person who tended to initially reject proposals. He called Aakash and expressed his concerns, "Aakash, think carefully before leaving your current job. It's quite lucrative, and your office has provided you with a flat in a prestigious area. Setting up your own business will take time and hard work. Running a business is no easy task. Please take your time to decide." With that, he hung up.

Pine and Aakash followed through with their plans, resigning from their respective jobs and giving notice at their offices, which had a waiting period of three months. During this time, Aakash visited Jaipur over a weekend to inspect the chosen office space, which Pine's father had already reviewed.

Upon completing the transition, they shifted to Jaipur, embarking on their new business venture. They selected an office location near the city center and designed the office layout. Additionally, they began the process of hiring employees by advertising for vacant positions.

Within a month, they initiated interviews and successfully hired five employees, marking the commencement of their new business. Pine herself took charge of the firm's marketing process. To finance the venture, they utilized some of their mutual funds and secured the remaining capital through a bank loan. The initial two years were challenging, particularly in meeting employee salaries and rent payments. Pine's father, Mr. Ranvir, extended financial support as needed. On the other hand, Aakash's parents were displeased with the decisions and occasionally attributed the decisions to their daughter-in-law, Pine.

After four years, their firm was thriving, and they expanded their workforce significantly. During this time, their daughter began attending school. Pine approached her father, suggesting that he sell his land in Himachal Pradesh to her. Mr. Ranvir inquired, "Why should I sell the land? If you have a plan, go ahead and execute it."

Pine responded, "Papa, I don't want to appear unfair to my two sisters. They might think that as the eldest sister, I have laid claim to your land. That's why I'm requesting you to sell the land to me."

In response, Ranvir proposed, "If this sentiment is important to you, let's convene a family dinner tonight at my place and discuss this matter openly in front of everyone.

In the evening, Pine and her family gathered at her parent's house for dinner. Before dinner, Mr. Ranvir addressed the family, saying, "I've called you all here tonight for a specific reason. Pine expressed her desire to purchase the land in Himachal Pradesh from me, fearing that her sisters may perceive her as selfish or dishonest."

Pine chimed in, "Yes, Papa. It's just a matter of time before Pony has her baby, and I wouldn't want them to think ill of me."

Mr. Ranvir continued, "Well, I've decided to lease the land to you for ten years. At the end of the lease period, you'll have the option to either return the land to me or purchase it. If this proposal suits everyone, I'll be pleased."

The family members were content with this arrangement. Himani inquired, "Pine, why the urgency for the land? Is there a particular plan?"

Pine approached her mother, embracing her, and said, "Yes, Maa, I intend to establish an apple orchard and a sizable fruit farm on that land."

Moved by the sentiment, Himani's eyes welled up, and she hugged her daughter tightly before heading inside. After dinner, everyone returned to their respective homes.

Within a week, Pine and Aakash traveled to Himachal Pradesh to put their plan into action. Through diligent work, they planted 1000 two-year-old apple trees on the land. They also sought guidance from a horticulture specialist, Mr. Manoj Upadhyay, to ensure the optimal and swift growth of their apple orchard.

Mr. Manoj provided valuable insights, saying, "Cultivating plants, plant breeding, crop production, particularly apple, and plant physiology are essential aspects. Since you've planted two-year-old trees, for early production, it's crucial to choose fast-growing varieties. You're fortunate to have planted them during the spring season, which is ideal. I'd recommend that you maintain consistent care and meticulous attention, with a primary focus on disease prevention. Any slightly spoiled apples can be processed into apple jam in a factory."

Today, Pine stands as the leading apple producer and seller in the region. Her dedication and hard work have earned her recognition from the Chief Minister, who expressed gratitude to Pine's husband, Aakash, for his unwavering support. The Chief Minister commended Pine for her initiative in involving young women from nearby villages, who have since built prosperous lives in Himachal Pradesh. Pine, the first CA to transition into orchard management, now possesses an extensive knowledge of various apple varieties. This entrepreneurial venture served as the foundation for her remarkable success as a woman.

A Leading Lady, Pony

Every name carries significance. When naming their first daughter, Pine, their father may not have delved deeply into the meaning of her name, but rather chosen a name that complemented the firstborn.

Years later, when Pony was pregnant, she found herself engrossed in a painting of her favorite sport, horseback riding. As she painted, she pondered the significance of her own name, "Pony," which translates to a small horse. The essence of her name embodies the idea of being the "little one." While people sometimes mistake ponies for baby horse foals, the two are distinct but serve unique purposes in the world. Despite their smaller stature, ponies are sturdy and hardworking animals, displaying a remarkable capacity to endure harsh weather conditions.

Ponies are known for their intelligence, making them suitable for a variety of tasks, from riding to pulling and even racing. Their smaller size often appeals to individuals of shorter stature, making them an ideal choice for riding.

The name 'Pony' was not bestowed without reason. It carries its own distinct personality and leaves a lasting impact on her life's journey.

Pony was lost in her thoughts, contemplating the meaning of her name. She realized that names are given to us at birth, shaping our personalities and the paths we'll follow in life. A name is an integral part of one's identity and can have an influence on their destiny or karma. While we may react to our karma, we cannot escape it. Certain life events are predetermined before birth, which is why it's said that we choose our parents. Our personalities follow a predetermined path once we're born. She collected her thoughts and concluded that she couldn't change her personality at this point. She embraced the fact that Pony was an intelligent and unique part of her identity.

During her college days at JJ College of Architecture in Mumbai, Pony met Ajay. Despite being from the same city, they hadn't crossed paths until college. Their interactions began with arguments and disagreements. Pony had two close friends, Mitali and Payal, who were also her roommates. They explored the city together. Mitali hailed from Amritsar, Punjab, while Payal came from a village near Varanasi.

The first semester came to a close, marked by their ongoing arguments. With only a brief break before the second semester, many students chose not to return to their hometowns. Instead, they explored nearby places, with some heading to Goa. Pony and her two friends opted to stay in Mumbai, spending their days discovering the city's intriguing sights.

Mumbai, known as the financial capital of India, is a densely populated city with a plethora of interesting places to explore. At the start of their vacation, Pony and her three friends decided to visit the Gateway of India. From there, they planned a day trip to the Elephanta Caves, located on Elephanta Island, which is home to ancient cave temples dedicated to Lord Shiva. To get there, they took a one-hour ferry ride that departed from the Gateway of India. They also visited the Haji Ali Dargah on a different day.

On a Tuesday, they made plans to visit the Siddhivinayak Temple, dedicated to Lord Ganesh, situated in Prabhadevi, Mumbai.

After the first semester, it became known that Pony had scored the highest marks in some papers, while Ajay had excelled in others, falling just three marks behind Pony. During a break, Ajay and his friends, Vijay and Jayesh, approached Pony and playfully teased them. Pony grew irate and remarked, "I know why they are teasing us. I believe they're disappointed because we outperformed them. We've put in hard work, which is why we achieved good marks."

Ajay responded, "We also earned good marks, but these girls are showing ego to prove that they are better than us. We'll see next time." This interaction highlighted the opposing dynamics between Pony and Ajay, leading to further disagreements in the corridors when they crossed paths.

After the second semester, Pony booked her ticket on the Aravali Express, leaving from Mumbai Central in the evening. Her other two friends had also booked their train tickets for the same day. Pony arrived at the station an hour ahead of the departure time. The train was punctual, and she boarded the air-conditioned coach. As the train left on time, Pony thought about how convenient it was and that she would reach home as scheduled.

Pony settled into her lower berth and was taken aback when she noticed Ajay sitting in the same coach, across from her. She feigned ignorance of his presence. But as soon as Ajay saw Pony, he quipped, "Thorns will never leave roses anywhere. Roses and thorns keep overlapping each other every time."

Pony responded with a hint of sarcasm, "I don't know how ants manage to find sugar everywhere. They follow the sugar trail closely," as she gave Ajay a sharp look.

During a stop at Kalyan station, two young men boarded the train and took seats near Pony. When it was around 10 o'clock, Pony politely asked these men to vacate her seat since she had the lower berth, and it was late at night.

One of the men retorted, "Oh, it's time to sleep!" and let out a sarcastic laugh.

Pony chose not to respond and remained seated. Then, one of the men nudged her, causing Ajay to become visibly agitated. He firmly told the men, "Show respect to the lady. She's the only female passenger in this cabin."

The man replied with a disrespectful comment, "Why are you so bothered? Is she your girlfriend?"

Ajay issued a stern warning, "If you two are educated, you should conduct yourselves properly in the presence of a lady."

To this, the man arrogantly retorted, "Why is the lady traveling alone? We have every right to touch and tease her. We could even buy her."

"Buy her? Is the lady a commodity?" Ajay began arguing with the two men. He firmly stated, "I won't tolerate any disrespectful remarks about her; she's my fiancée." With that, Ajay moved closer to Pony and sat between the two men. Fortunately, the train ticket checker arrived at that moment.

Pony complained to the ticket checker about the inappropriate behavior of the two men and requested a seat change for them.

On the train, Pony and Ajay's love story began to unfold. Upon reaching Jaipur, they exchanged phone numbers and addresses.

Pony's father, Ranvir, came to pick her up from the station. During the car ride, Pony narrated the incident on the train and expressed her gratitude, saying, "Dad, Ajay helped me a lot during the journey."

Once they arrived home, Pony looked up Ajay's address and discovered that his family owned a chain of hotels in Jaipur and Rajasthan.

In the evening, Ajay called Pony and asked her to meet him at the mall. During their meeting, both of them apologized to each other, even though they weren't entirely sure why they were apologizing. In the café, Ajay reached out and held her hand, saying, "Pony, I love you. The day I first saw you in class, I felt an inexplicable connection, as if we've known each other for many lifetimes. We've crossed paths in countless places. Haven't you felt it?"

Pony burst into laughter and replied, "Are you kidding, Ajay? Many lives? We met in college for the first time, and honestly, I had no idea how you felt about me. You seemed to dislike me, always teasing and arguing with me. I even thought you were jealous when I got the top rank in the first semester."

"Now that all the arguments and fights are behind us, Pony, I want to tell you how much I love you," said Ajay. "I'll introduce you to my younger sister, Mita, who is just a year and two months younger than me."

Pony, filled with curiosity, asked, "I've seen your hotels online. How many hotels do you have? Are they all in Jaipur? Who manages them?"

Responding with a smile, Ajay inquired, "So many questions today? Today, please tell me that you love me as much as I love you."

After her meeting with Ajay at the café, Pony returned home. It was the first time someone had directly proposed to her. That night, sleep eluded her. She contemplated the meaning of love, believing it to be divine and capable of bringing happiness rather than pain. Love was a blissful emotion. Pony couldn't sleep that night as she pondered why Ajay had behaved rudely toward her in class despite his feelings.

Two days later, when Pony was heading to meet Ajay, she asked her sister Ride to accompany her to the mall. Ride, smiling, inquired, "Why the sudden trip to the mall? What's going on? I noticed something, Mej (second sister). You've been losing sleep and not eating properly lately. What's bothering you?"

Pony and Ride went to the nearby mall, where, after about ten minutes, Ajay arrived with his sister Mita. Pony introduced Ride to Ajay, who in turn introduced his younger sister, saying, "This is my sister, Mita. She's in twelfth grade."

Pony added, "My sister Ride is also in twelfth grade, and she aspires to become a doctor. She's an exceptionally bright student."

After returning home, both Ride and Pony sat on the terrace. Ride expressed, "Mej, I really like your choice, and his sister is also lovely. I'm heading downstairs for my tuition class now."

Pony gazed at the night sky, pondering thoughts she'd read in the book "Where Love Begins, Vibhavari" : "In love, blood relations and relatives are not significant. Love isn't defined by romantic touches, physical warmth, movies, or park outings. It's about caring, respect, understanding, and unwavering trust. Love is mental peace. I distinctly remember the best line from the book: 'Love is blissful, divine, and spiritual. Love is freedom.'"

The next day, Ajay called Pony and asked for a favorable response. He expressed over the phone, "Please come and meet me in the park near your house. I've already told you how much I love you. Love you! And love you! Come at 5:00 in the evening."

Pony's heart raced as she listened to Ajay's voice, and beads of perspiration formed on her forehead. At five, she informed Ride that she was going to meet Ajay. Pony arrived at the park on time, contemplating how to respond to Ajay. She sat on a bench in the park, lost in thought, and then, suddenly, saw Ajay standing behind her. He gently touched her shoulder and said, "Pony, I love you."

Pony's head bowed, and she felt a sense of embarrassment and shame. She admitted, "I don't know what to say. If others find out about our relationship, they'll ask many questions. My elder sister is a very modest girl, just a year and a half older than me. She's pursuing her CA and is a dedicated student."

Ajay replied, "I'm not concerned about your elder sister or family matters right now. I want your answer today."

Pony sighed and responded, "Why the hurry? You don't understand the complexities girls face."

"Yes, darling! I'm in a hurry to know the answer because I want to introduce you to my family soon," Ajay explained.

Pony nodded and confessed, "Yes, I love you now, Ajay. But back in college, I initially disliked you because you always seemed to tease me. However, when I met you on the train, my opinion completely changed, especially after you protected me from those obnoxious passengers."

They then went to a nearby restaurant and relished their time together. Pony shared a memory of their father, who had always been a source of encouragement and motivation. She recalled, "Our father was incredible. Once, when he used to drop my sister (Pine) at her coaching class, he noticed a boy who always seemed to be around her. One day, he approached that boy, asked his name, and inquired about his pursuits. The boy explained that he was attending a coaching class for the joint entrance exam in engineering. Our father kindly handed him a card and told him to meet up after he completed his engineering. Later, we found out that he had fallen in love with one of his classmates in engineering. Our father was never unkind to anyone; he was our inspiration for facing life's challenges."

After three more years, they graduated with honors in Architecture and contemplated pursuing their master's degrees. Both were selected in the campus interviews by reputable companies. However, while Pony got a job in Vadodara, Ajay was selected for a different location. Pony worked in Vadodara for two months but became homesick, so she returned to Jaipur. Her father, Ranvir, reassured her, "Pon, you don't need to go back to Vadodara. We can explore opportunities here."

Ajay also decided to leave his job and come back to Jaipur. His father, Mr. Paresh Baghel, was a hotelier with five hotels in Jaipur and Rajasthan. Ajay's mother, Janki, was thrilled to have her son back and suggested to Paresh, "You should ask Ajay to join you in the hotel business."

Ajay approached his father with a request to build an additional unit in their Jaipur hotel. Paresh, his father, suggested the possibility of constructing a unit in Udaipur due to available open spaces in the area. Ajay believed that involving Pony in their work would be beneficial. When Paresh inquired about Pony, Ajay explained, "Pony is my best friend from my college in Mumbai. She is very talented and achieved the highest scores in our college. Together, we can make this unit exceptional."

Paresh agreed, saying, "If you both believe you can accomplish wonders, I don't mind calling her. Discuss the compensation and perks with her."

Ajay shared his plan with Pony, who was interested in the opportunity but concerned about seeking her family's permission.

Upon discovering Ajay's idea, Pony approached her father during a supper together. She said, "Papa, I've received a job offer in Udaipur and need to start next week."

Mr. Agarwal, who never denied his daughters' proposals, responded, "Very well, I'll drop you off in Udaipur next week."

Pony hesitated and decided to discuss it further with Ajay. The next day, she arranged a meeting between Ajay and her father. She called Ajay to her father's textile office, where they had an introduction.

Ajay arrived promptly, and Pony introduced him to her father, Mr. Ranvir Agarwal. Mr. Agarwal was pleased with Ajay's polite demeanor and did not inquire about him further.

That evening, Mr. Agarwal asked Pony, "I didn't ask Ajay about his background. Where does he live in Jaipur, and tell me more about his family."

Pony replied, "Ajay's father runs a hotel business with properties all over Rajasthan. They have a chain of hotels to their name. Ajay and his sister, Mita, live with their family in Vaishali Nagar, Jaipur. Mita is in the final year of engineering. While I haven't met their family yet, I've had several interactions with Mita."

Mr. Agarwal suggested, "Before you leave for Udaipur, can't our family meet his family?"

Pony responded, "I'm not sure, Papa, but I'll discuss it with Ajay."

Subsequently, the two families arranged a meeting. Ajay's grandparents, Shri Pravin Baghel and Smt. Satyavati, invited Pony's family to their home in Vaishali Nagar.

Ranvir's family decided that after Pine's marriage, they would begin making arrangements for Pony's wedding. With this in mind, Pony and Ajay set off for Udaipur to embark on their new project. Before their departure, Mr. Paresh Baghel asked Ajay about the project's timeline and expenses. He also wanted to know if Ajay had organized everything necessary for the endeavor. While confident in his son's capabilities, Mr. Baghel was eager to hear Ajay's plan.

"Dad, to answer your first question, I plan to complete the project within two years at the latest. Secondly, I've already scheduled a meeting with the bank, which is set for tomorrow. I'll be meeting with Mr. Parekh. Dad, I kindly request you to accompany us. Your vast experience and humility are highly respected in Jaipur," said Ajay.

Mr. Baghel and Ajay were ready to go by 10 in the morning. When they arrived at the meeting point, Mr. Baghel inquired about Pony's absence, wondering if she was running late.

"No, Dad. Pony will be going directly to the bank. She's just feeling a little apprehensive, as this new situation has made her a bit shy," explained Ajay.

Ajay's father responded, "It's natural for people to feel shy when they're uncertain about how to act or react in a new business environment, but Pony is a smart young lady. She knows what she's doing."

Upon arriving at the bank, the trio noticed Pony waiting near the entrance.

"She's not only intelligent and beautiful but also punctual and disciplined," commented Mr. Baghel.

The three of them proceeded to the bank manager's office. Mr. Baghel introduced Ajay and Pony to Mr. Parekh. Observing Mr. Baghel's reputation and assets, the bank manager promptly approved a substantial loan in Ajay's name.

Ajay requested the bank manager and his father to include Pony's name on the loan documents since both were actively involved in the new project. With the loan granted swiftly, they decided to head to the site of the new hotel immediately.

Within a week, they made their way to Udaipur, taking up residence in one of Ajay's nearby hotels. The plot of land for their new project was right next door. Excited, Pony and Ajay explored the area and were thrilled with the site of their dream hotel. As architects, they quickly drafted plans for a double-storeyed hotel, envisioning a small lake just outside the building, surrounded by a flower garden and shaded by large trees on all sides. The forested area extended to the boundaries, which delighted Pony.

Their love life took a back seat as both of them wholeheartedly focused on their project. At times, they got so engrossed that they even forgot to have lunch. The hotel manager ensured that their meals were sent to the building site, as per Mr. Paresh Baghel's instructions.

Civil engineers, some of whom were Ajay's former classmates, were consulted before they arrived at the site. They tentatively estimated that it would take approximately two years to complete the entire project.

Laborers were hired for the excavation of the lake, and within a month, the small lake was ready. Pony provided guidance to the female laborers, directing them to plant trees, rose shrubs, and a variety of attractive flowers in the garden near the lake. Despite the immense effort required, they successfully planted all the plants within two days. Marble garden benches were placed around the lake. Pony also took the initiative to clean the forested area right up to the boundaries.

Two years later, their dream hotel was completed, and Ajay and Pony were brimming with enthusiasm and excitement at having achieved their dream.

A year ago, Pine got married and settled in Mumbai. Pony spent a week in Mumbai to attend her sister's wedding.

Currently, both Ajay and Pony had returned to Jaipur for some time to spend with their respective families. Mr. Baghel reached out to Mr. Agarwal to arrange a date for their marriage. Ajay suggested to Pony, "Dear, we haven't had a day exclusively to ourselves. How about spending three to four hours together? We could go for a long drive and enjoy our time together." Pony eagerly agreed.

As they embarked on their long drive, Pony expressed her desire to recite a poem she had written during the challenging journey of fulfilling their dream.

Love

My heart knows the value of invaluable Love,
Pray, God consummated my life with stewpot!
One birth I met you with love tight knot,
All birth I tight you hug and float all above.

Goodness of Love, as joy will Rise,
The wonder of the Wise.
Love is God's amazing Act,
This life is a lovely Fact.

True love is knowing Me,
Thus, wisdom in each other's Glee.
Contentment in love is Bliss,
Not losing and never Miss.

Love is happiness Within,
No physical attachments Seen.
In search of lovely Soulmate,
This achievement in love is Great.

After reciting the poem, Pony said, "I cannot recite this poem in front of everyone, so I decided to share it with you one day."

Two months later, Ajay and Pony's wedding date was finalized, and they tied the knot in November. Panditji Bharadwajji presided over the ceremony, guiding the couple through the traditional marriage rituals, including the Saptapadi.

For their honeymoon, they chose to spend two days at their project site. During this time, they named their budding product "ANY," signifying "A" for Ajay and the last two letters of Pony's name.

Within those two days, Pony suggested adding ponies and horses to the hotel's amenities. They initially planned to establish a stable with at least ten ponies and two horses. Pony told Ajay, "Once we're back in Jaipur, we must advertise horse and pony riding at the 'ANY' hotel in Udaipur."

During their two-day honeymoon, love and long drives refreshed their minds, making them both happy.

Guests began flocking to the ANY hotel, especially for the riding experiences. Many people preferred ponies due to their height, while taller individuals opted for horseback riding. The riding tours commenced from the stable, taking guests from the lake through the forest and extending to the hotel's boundaries. It wasn't long before they had to expand their stable facilities, creating separate spaces for ponies and horses.

Within five years, their riding business generated substantial revenue. The Revenue Minister of Rajasthan invited Pony, Ajay, and their adorable baby girl, Piu, to his office for dinner. He commended their impressive success in just five years, acknowledging Ajay's father, Mr. Baghel, for his longstanding business presence. The minister expressed hope that the region would soon attract many foreign tourists.

In response, Pony shared, "My name is Pony Agarwal. Many relatives and neighbors used to tease me because of my name, but I always felt proud. My father chose this name, considering ponies' intelligence. We three sisters are proud of our father for naming us Pine, Pony, and Ride. People may think these names lack meaning, but I believe that our names are reflections of our karma, and our personalities grow from the names we are given."

Pony reiterated the same sentiment when the state's Revenue Minister invited their family to a dinner party. The audience in the auditorium applauded while listening to Pony, and the Revenue Minister was delighted to have Pony's family as his guests in the evening.

Love Story Of Ride

Every year, Pine, Pony, and Ride visited their bungalow in Kasol. During one of their visits, Ride and Ria decided to stay in Kasol for a few extra days. It was during this time that Ride met Paramjeet in the market, and her world suddenly felt different. She struggled to sleep, tossing and turning in bed. Ride wondered, "Is this love? I've only known him for a few days, so why is this happening now? Why is my mind so restless and indecisive today? Why do I keep thinking about him constantly? I stayed awake until 2:00 a.m., but what's the reason behind all this?" She remembered her friend Priya, who had recently gotten married and told her that her feelings had changed drastically after getting engaged. Ride could now relate to what Priya had experienced.

The following morning, she asked Ria, "Have you read 'Where Love Begins Vibhavari,' a love story?"

Ria replied, "Yes, I read the book and found some definitions of love in it. Love is described as divine. It never brings pain to the mind; it always brings happiness. Love is blissful."

Ride's mental turmoil persisted as she met Paramjeet in the market. Concerned for her friend, Ria suggested, "Let's go to the market again today."

That evening, Ria and Ride returned to the Kasol market but couldn't find Paramjeet. They decided to visit their grandfather Prasad Nirmal's house. They reached the house in fifteen minutes and knocked on the door. When Ride saw Paramjeet opening the door, her heart raced, and she found it hard to speak when entering the house.

Ria asked Paramjeet, "If you don't mind, can we go to the market for a while?"

Prasad uncle agreed, saying, "Jeet, you can take them out to explore the area since they'll be visiting often now. They should get to know the place."

After changing his clothes, Paramjeet accompanied them to the market. Ria explained to him, "You know, her mental state has been quite unstable. She couldn't talk to anyone at home, and all she says is that she's feeling something in her heart. The day she met you in the market, when they all left for Jaipur, Ride and I stayed here for a few more days. Every day, we came to the market hoping to find you but were disappointed. Today, we were determined to meet you no matter what. We even decided to visit grandfather's house."

"What's the matter? I can tell something has been bothering you. Isn't that right, Ride?" Paramjeet inquired.

Ride nodded and replied, "I don't know why, but can you please share your phone number with me? Also, how long will you be here?"

"Don't be in such a hurry; I'll give you my phone number," Paramjeet said.

At 7:00 in the evening, Ria and Ride returned to the bungalow. At 8:00, Ride asked Ria, "Should I call him now? I know he probably won't call me. I understand he might not have any interest or feelings for me, but he doesn't know what's happening to me."

Ria encouraged her, saying, "You should call him and tell him how you feel. If he doesn't feel the same, the most he can say is 'no.' But you must be mentally prepared for that."

Ride called Paramjeet, but when he answered, she couldn't utter a word, and the phone disconnected.

Ria scolded her, saying, "Why didn't you say anything, Ride? If you get so nervous, how will you become a gynaecologist?"

Ride retorted, "I know you're making fun of me. Let's see how you handle it if you fall in love in the future. Now it's your turn to be unkind to me. Anyway, this time, I'll be direct with him."

Ride called Paramjeet again, but this time she was composed. She confessed, "Paramjeet, I love you. You may not have any feelings for me, but I'm asking you to hear me out. Since the day I met you in the market, I've had these feelings. My mind and sleep have been in turmoil."

Paramjeet replied gently, "Wait, wait! You're so eloquent with your feelings. In an Army family, we may come across as a bit rough, but we also have love, affection, and warmth for our fellow countrymen."

Ride urged him, "Please, don't hang up. Just listen to me."

"I don't have the courage to say 'no.' Please go on," Paramjeet said.

Ride continued, "Love isn't like camphor, extinguishing in a few seconds and turning black. Have you ever been to the seashores of Mumbai or Goa? If you stand there during a sunset or sunrise, you can see the sun either disappearing beneath the water or emerging from it. We gaze at the horizon, a distance we can't measure. Love is similar; it knows no boundaries."

Paramjeet added, "I've been to the seashores of Goa and Puri, Odisha many times."

"Wind, clouds, rain, sunshine—all these elements are interconnected. Love forms a relationship like them, bearing many similarities with these four things," Ride explained.

She continued, "Imagine putting a pencil point on paper and drawing a continuous circle. Eventually, you can't connect the first and last points with your fingers. That profound feeling is what we call love."

Paramjeet remained silent, attentively listening to Ride's explanation about love.

"Have you ever noticed lines of ants moving in opposite directions, meeting, and kissing as they draw near? That's love," Ride explained.

Laughter erupted from the other end of the phone. "Ants? Don't laugh."

"Don't laugh," Ride insisted. "Have you ever observed the courtship of pigs?"

"Pigs? Hahaha!"

"Tonight, you have to listen to my thoughts on love," Ride insisted.

"Why do rivers flow towards the sea, making sounds? It's because they long to meet their love—the sea or the ocean. If you keep an open heart and mind, you'll see love everywhere. No one has witnessed the exact moment when flowers bloom, but we see bees transferring pollen from one to another. Even plants, dependent on each other, understand the meaning of love."

"Male peacocks dance, shaking and shimmering their feathers in a way that creates a mesmerizing display of flickering feathers and distinctive sounds. This is how they call for courtship and display their vitality to female peacocks. If you open your senses, you'll find love everywhere. Even male cuckoos sing for females. Here I am, a female, explaining everything to a male."

"Hello, are you still there?" Ride called out over the phone. "Love isn't just about romantic intimacy, going to the movies, or taking walks in serene places. It's about caring, sacrifice, understanding, respect, and, above all, trust. Love is a search for mental peace in life."

Paramjeet replied, "Tomorrow morning, around ten, I'll come to your bungalow with my response. I want to discuss many things with you."

At 10 o'clock the following morning, Paramjeet rang the doorbell. Ride and Ria were eagerly waiting for him. They thought about having breakfast together. After the meal, Ria told Ride, "I'm going to explore the beauty of this place. You talk to him and finalize the relationship."

Ria bid farewell, leaving Ride alone with Paramjeet. He handed her an envelope, and Ride asked, "What's in the envelope, and why are you giving it to me?"

Paramjeet replied, "Why are you anxious about the envelope? Open it and see what's inside."

With trembling hands, Ride opened the envelope, wondering why, as a doctor, her hands were shaking so badly.

"I don't know what Love is.

I know one thing,

You are above all things.

I never felt in my heart anything,

Until you met me for something.

I do not know that is Love or not,

I have a heart sinking feeling for you.

After opening the envelope, Ride found these lines on a watermark letterhead. She said, "I feel fortunate to have you in my life, and I'm delighted that you've accepted my love. When I first saw and met you in the market, I had a strong feeling that you were the man I've been waiting for. Now, I'd like to share that I'm in my final semester of medical school at Pilani. After completing my MBBS, I intend to specialize in gynecology. I'll soon be appearing for the entrance exam for my MD. How about you?"

"Since my childhood, I've been raised in an Army family. All my relatives are in the military. So, I've been preparing for the National Defence Academy (NDA) after completing my 12th grade. The NDA is the joint defense service training institute for the Indian Armed Forces, where cadets from the Indian Army, Indian Navy, and Indian Air Force train together before moving on to their respective service academies for further pre-commission training. I was fortunate to be selected on my first attempt and studied in Pune, Maharashtra, India. Cadets undergo comprehensive training, covering all aspects of military and academics over three years. I'm currently posted in Shimla, which is closer to this area, allowing me to visit my grandfather frequently.

When Paramjeet accepted Ride's proposal, both were overjoyed. Within a week, Ria and Ride left Kasol.

"Love can't be bought from a market. Have you ever seen a pearl? Not all oysters contain pearls, and finding one is quite challenging. Love is equally precious and often as hard to discover as a pearl. After completing my school life and now in medical college, I've finally found my love," Ride said, smiling, during a phone call with Paramjeet.

When Paramjeet mentioned, "I believe I've been searching for this person for several lifetimes," it moved her to tears.

Ride excelled in her MBBS with flying colors and secured admission to AIIMS for specialization in gynecology. Ria enrolled in another college in Chandigarh, Punjab, India.

Paramjeet visited Delhi AIIMS multiple times, and they often met on the college campus. On one occasion, Paramjeet took Ride to explore the military cantonment in Delhi, where some of his friends were posted. When she was in her final year, Ranvir, her father, met Paramjeet, as Ride had informed her father when she fell in love with Paramjeet in Kasol. Ranvir knew that he had purchased the bungalow from Paramjeet's grandfather.

After discussions with Paramjeet's family, their marriage was arranged. Paramjeet's elder brother, Lt. Pravin Nirmal, was stationed in Punjab. Being in the Army, Paramjeet's father, Mr. Abhijeet Nirmal, was a jovial individual. The wedding was scheduled during Paramjeet's posting in Dehradun, Uttarakhand, India. Following her post-graduation, Ride joined the military hospital in Dehradun. For their honeymoon, they visited Goa, fulfilling Ride's desire to witness both sunrise and sunset together with her loved one.

In Goa, as they went to witness the sunset, she pointed out the horizon and said, "Look at the horizon. My love for you is as vast and endless as that horizon," and hugged him tightly. On their way back from the beach, Ride playfully mentioned, "Have you ever seen the love-making of pigs? It's surprisingly similar to humans. They kiss, hug, and then engage in lovemaking." Both of them shared a hearty laugh and returned to their hotel.

Upon reaching the hotel, Ride emerged from the bathroom and informed Param, "I've got my period (menstruation)."

"Take some rest," Param assured her.

"Param, let me share an incident from when I was in the eighth grade," Ride began. "My father used to pick us up from school every day. One afternoon, after we left school, Papa asked Mej (Pony) to escort me to the school restroom. Pony took me there, and that's when I got my first period. On the way home, Papa explained everything about menstruation in a scientific and matter-of-fact way. He even mentioned that unless there's severe discomfort, we can participate in meditation, including visiting temples and cultural events. He emphasized that menstruation is a natural bodily function, just like the excretion we do daily. Our father is not just a parent but also our mother, guide, mentor, and best friend."

Telling this story moved Ride emotionally. Param came close and reassured her, saying, "I'm here with you for seven lifetimes to take care of you."

The following morning, they returned to Jaipur for Pagphere (a ritual observed eight days after the wedding). After a two-day stay in Jaipur, they went back to Paramjeet's house in Shimla. A week later, both Ride and Paramjeet resumed their respective work placements.

A year later, Ride became pregnant, and Paramjeet received a transfer to a remote location. Despite their physical separation, they stayed in touch every night. As Ride's delivery date approached, Paramjeet's parents arrived in Dehradun to be with her. Ride gave birth to a baby boy, whom they named Jaideep. Paramjeet was occupied with his work and couldn't be present for the birth of their son. He managed to visit them for a day when the baby was two months old. During the visit, Paramjeet expressed, "I'm overjoyed to see my little boy. People say the sky is the limit, but I say, love knows no limits. It transcends even the boundless sky. I envision love when I'm alone at my remote posting."

The next day, Paramjeet had to return to his posting location. Six months later, news broke on television that an officer's camp had been attacked by terrorists. Seven officers were having dinner at the camp when gunfire suddenly erupted. Two officers were severely injured, and the rest sustained bullet wounds in their arms or legs. These seven officers, who were unprepared for the attack, managed to apprehend two terrorists alive at the camp.

Upon hearing this news on TV, Ride rushed to the army office to get accurate information. She learned that a helicopter had reached the remote location, and all the injured personnel were transported to the nearest hospital. Tragically, two officers lost their lives as a result of their injuries and were honored as martyrs.

Upon hearing the news, Ride comforted her parents-in-law and said, "I'm heading to the office now to check on Param's condition. If possible, I will inquire about having him transferred to this hospital. I'll also see if he can speak to us on the phone. Maa, please look after Deep. I'll call you once I reach the hospital." Her father-in-law, Mr. Pravin Nirmal, accompanied Ride to the hospital.

Upon reaching the hospital, Ride and Pravinji learned that all the officers were not in a condition to be shifted to Dehradun. They had received initial treatment in the local hospital, and they would be transferred to the nearest military hospital the following day. The treatment would take time.

After five months of treatment, when Paramjeet was brought back to Dehradun, Ride, her father-in-law, and mother-in-law were devastated to discover that he had undergone amputation of one leg. This life-altering experience affected his mobility, ability to work, pursue his profession, and maintain his independence. The constant pain and emotional trauma complicated Param's recovery.

The decision to amputate a limb to save the life of an army officer was a horrifying experience. Handling the situation was challenging for Ride and her family. When a loved one suffered, Ride realized that it was a whole different matter, despite her experience as a doctor in dealing with critical situations in the hospital.

Ride's parents, Ranvir and Himani, came to meet their traumatized daughter upon Paramjeet's return to Dehradun. Ride had saved many lives in the hospital, but now she faced the difficulty of dealing with a loved one's suffering. However, with the grace of God, Param, with the help of crutches, began to move. Ride provided him with inspiration and care, and he gradually regained his mobility. Within a year, Paramjeet had to retire from the Army. While Ride could have occupied army quarters due to her job at the military hospital, she chose to resign and open a private practice in Dehradun.

Ride reassured Param, saying, "Our love is unbreakable, Param. I found you, and our connection is so strong that no external force can sever it. We are like a concrete building, not a fragile hut. No matter how many storms come, our love remains intact."

Paramjeet replied by hugging Ride, "I know, Ride. Our love is powerful, and you are my strength. When you're by my side, I'm as strong as a mountain, ready to protect myself and our family."

Dr. Ride's clinic soon gained popularity in Dehradun. She transitioned from a small clinic to a maternity hospital and employed two other doctors initially. She became renowned for her expertise in insemination and IVF programs, using concentrated sperm directly in the uterus around the time of ovulation.

Dr. Ride also incorporated homeopathic treatments for women struggling with infertility, drawing on knowledge passed down from her grandmother, who had used homeopathic remedies to treat local residents. Dr. Ride recalled her grandmother's homeopathic medicine kit and its effectiveness in her practice.

The objective of this treatment is to enhance the chances of fertilization by increasing the number of healthy sperm that reach the fallopian tubes during a woman's most fertile period. Frequently, her junior doctors and nurses inquired about the name of the medicine she used. She would explain, "It's a homeopathic medicine with no side effects. In homeopathy, symptoms are crucial, and doctors must listen attentively to the patient. Even details like thirst are essential."

Two vital medicines she prescribed were "Medorinum 1000," used for women with fatty genital conditions or those with rheumatoid arthritis, and "Konium," for women with narrow passages in the uterus. These medicines were employed when women experienced issues with the uterus, fallopian tubes, or ovaries. Initially, sperm were tested in the pathology department, and if the sperm were healthy, the women were treated by Dr. Ride.

Within two years, patients from villages and distant places learned about Dr. Ride's hospital. She became exceptionally well-known in the city, and her frequent write-ups on infertility attracted those in the medical field.

Upon returning home one day, Ride was warmly embraced by Paramjeet. He said, "Your dream has finally come true, my darling! I remember when you were at AIIMS; you shared this vision with me. You wanted to ensure no woman's lap remains empty, protecting them from societal judgments as 'infecund (barren) ladies.' I always knew your love would succeed one day."

At the dinner table, Ride told Param, "I know that with you by my side every step of the way, no external force can deter me from pursuing my goals."

While administering his medicine, Ride approached Param's chair, and he couldn't hold back his tears. He said, "My class is ready, my love! Starting next week, I will begin training students for the NDA (National Defence Academy). Ten students have already enrolled at a minimal fee."

Ride replied, "I'm overjoyed today. Your dream world is finally within reach. It's not far from becoming a reality."

One year later, when Dr. Ride entered her hospital, the nurses cheered, "Jai ho! Jai ho!" She was puzzled. Nurse Priti explained, "Doctor, today the Chief Minister visited our hospital to meet you. Since he found you weren't here yet, he handed us an envelope and instructed us to give it to you. We all know what's inside." Dr. Ride opened the envelope and found an invitation to a program the next day at an auditorium near the clock tower.

During that year, Paramjeet's classes had gained immense popularity in the city, especially among underprivileged students.

On the day of the event, Dr. Ride, Paramjeet, and their son Jaideep arrived on time. Their presence brought happiness to the venue. Both Ride and Paramjeet were well-known figures in the city, known for their humanitarian service. They charged minimal fees and sometimes waived them for the less fortunate.

At 4 in the evening, the Chief Minister entered and took the stage, where four chairs were placed. Four guests were called up, and Dr. Ride's name was announced. The CM presented her with the prestigious "Super Doctor Award" along with a cash prize intended for the development of her esteemed hospital. The CM expressed hopes that Dr. Ride would soon be nominated for the "Bidhan Chandra Roy" award, presented by the President of India annually in July. Paramjeet was also honored with a prestigious cap and a medal for his efforts to inspire young people to join the Indian Army, Indian Air Force, and Indian Navy.

The program concluded with the national anthem, resounding throughout the venue. Afterward, they proceeded to dinner with the CM and other distinguished personalities present at the function.

How To Get Ducks In A Row

Love and affection are two forces that can lead to recognition and acclaim. The understanding of love may vary from person to person, but its roots lie in trust, empathy, and care. The worth of love can be immeasurable, and it's crucial to recognize its value.

Mr. Agarwal had three daughters. When his three daughters were in school, he believed in their potential for remarkable achievements. He named them Pine, Pony, and Ride, thinking these names were devoid of meaning. The significance of Pine becomes apparent when we see a touch of green amidst a world blanketed in cold, white snow. The uniqueness of Pony is witnessed during a group of horses, with beautiful short ponies among them. Ride's importance is best appreciated when exploring picturesque landscapes.

Many relatives and people around him often urged Mr. Agarwal to have a son to carry on the family name. In response, he would say, "My daughters are both my sons and daughters. I don't adhere to age-old traditions. There's a reason behind God's plan."

He emphasized, "I love them dearly and have granted them the freedom to know that true love is founded on trust. I know they won't do anything to tarnish my reputation. Love and attachment are two distinct things that must be understood. Love is selfless, while attachment is a powerful binding force that often begins with the physical body, leading to other attachments. Love brings contentment; it is bliss and freedom that emanates from within. Love cannot be measured; it is felt rather than seen. It is not dependent on anything and doesn't involve arguments. Love is an emotion, a virtue, and can be described as an unselfish and humanitarian concern for others."

Mr. Ranvir believed that love is built on trust and trust is the foundation of love. He had placed his unwavering trust in his three daughters since their childhood, recognizing their talents. The ability to identify a child's talents is vital for parents.

The word "love" has multiple meanings in the dictionary, and many argue that love cannot be defined. Love can represent affection and, when one thinks of affection, it often conjures images of parental love for their children. Another aspect of love is fondness, associated with a liking for material possessions. Himani, Ranvir's wife, once wrote a poem on Affection:

"Love and affection are the same,

Believe two sides of a coin,

Two words have the same meaning,

One is universal and the other is restricted.

One gives the pleasure within,

Other gives the apathy to the mind.

One never can be measured,

One is restricted to the known".

Nowadays, Mr. Ranvir was immensely proud of his three daughters. He recalled the time when their births were met with criticism, but he remained steadfast in his belief. He shared, "Many years ago, when three goddesses were born into my family, I faced criticism from relatives who questioned the lack of sons in the family, citing concerns about family heirs. I was uncomfortable hearing such arguments within the family. I knew that when Pine was born, everyone had expected a baby boy. When Pony was born, there was little excitement initially, but within ten months, when she began walking, the entire neighborhood started making predictions. Nobody had visited the child when Ride was born. One day, I stumbled upon an article in a magazine about women."

The article stated, "Women are both the creators and preservers of society. Our society is replete with superstitions, and women continue these traditions. Women have the potential to build strong families and transform society into a better place by eliminating these superstitions. Women can create families, making society akin to heaven, by ridding it of these outdated beliefs."

The author of the article further discussed the importance of women in society, emphasizing the need for equality and mutual understanding between sons and daughters within the family. She questioned societal norms that imposed restrictions on women, such as wearing bangles and bindis only after marriage, and not applying the same standards to men. Her words urged women to initiate change by treating sons and daughters equally and nurturing values in society. The article emphasized that a mother's role as the first teacher is irreplaceable and crucial for societal development.

Indeed, women play a vital role in the growth of individuals from infancy to adulthood, from "Milk to Manhood," and it is the mother's influence that sets the foundation for one's values. The author concluded that women can shape society's outlook and must be responsible for its upliftment or downfall.

Oh! Women! Come hither, know yourself! Each one of you come closer and recognize your potential. Introspect within yourself and meditate deep into your ocean of talent. Forget the envy and make forgiveness your virtue. Shower your love and affection on all. Only then can you build a better and heavenly society.

Pine, Pony and Ride's father, Mr. Ranvir, knew that his daughters will be his assets one day. So, he used to read the articles on women. Sometimes, he used to read in front of his daughters and wife.

Before Navratri, he used to read the article on Maa Durga.

सर्व मंगल मांगल्ये, शिवे सर्वथ साधिके,
शरैन्ये त्रियाम्बके गौरी नारायणी नमःस्तुते

The final day of Pitripaksha is celebrated as Mahalaya, which falls on the Amavasya or new moon day of Ashwin (typically in September/October). This auspicious occasion is dedicated to invoking the Goddess of supreme power. Everyone eagerly awaits the nine days of Navratri, which begin the day after Mahalaya. During these nine days, it is believed that the powerful goddess will protect us from unwanted evils.

Durga Puja, one of the grandest festivals, is celebrated in early autumn. This festival is marked by a series of socio-cultural events that transcend social and economic divides. People from all walks of life eagerly prepare for this festival, with no distinctions of wealth or status. New clothes are purchased, adding to the festive spirit.

Navaratri is a time when we invoke the divine energy, embodied in the universal mother known as "Durga," which translates to the remover of life's miseries. She is also referred to as "Devi" (goddess) or "Shakti" (energy or power). This divine energy enables the divine to carry out the processes of creation, preservation, and destruction. In essence, we recognize that God is unchanging and motionless, while the Divine Mother Durga is the active force behind all creation. This concept aligns with the scientific principle that energy is imperishable, neither created nor destroyed, but always in existence.

Durga Puja has become one of the world's most celebrated festivals. The idols (Pratima) used in the worship are crafted from clay collected from courtyards that were once frequented by sex workers. This symbolism highlights how these women, often marginalized in society, contribute to saving society from malevolent forces, signifying that they play a role in safeguarding society from evils.

https://be-human.org/2007/10/17/durga-the-inner-power/

"I'm overjoyed today because I've always felt immense pride in my daughters. I had a strong belief that they would achieve remarkable feats one day. When the Himachal Pradesh Chief Minister acknowledged my daughter Pine's talent, I had a premonition that my other two daughters would also earn admiration in the future. Today, my other two daughters have become prominent figures in their respective fields," said Mr. Ranvir when asked to speak about his daughters' successes.

He continued, "Failure imparts invaluable lessons that success often cannot. Success and failure are intertwined like two sides of a coin. In philosophy, it's stated that the whole is comprised of numerous parts, with one being incomplete without the other. Day and night complement each other. In Buddhist philosophy, the concept of self and environment underscores the inseparability of life and its surroundings. Our external world, including our work and family relationships, reflects our inner selves. In Indian philosophy, Shiva and Shakti represent two facets of a singular truth – the negative and the positive, the abstract and the concrete, the male and the female. Genuine freedom and the discovery of inner talents flourish when parents recognize and nurture them during the formative years."

On another occasion, Mr. Agarwal invited the article's author, Shrimati Vidya Singh, to speak at an event and share her thoughts. She commenced by saying, "Some men fail to grasp the innate qualities and untapped potential within women. As a college professor, I used to believe that women were often reliant on men. However, a female student once enlightened me by stating that men, too, depend on women. She cited examples from her family, highlighting the contributions of her grandfather and father. It was an eye-opener, and I began to observe that, indeed, without women, men often struggle to make significant decisions within the family. As a member of a social organization, I've learned that married daughters are often the ones who call and stay connected with their parents, not their sons. I advocate for girls to retain their birth surnames even after marriage, instead of adopting their husband's surname exclusively. I believe that their children should carry both their father's and mother's surnames. If the surnames are too lengthy, they can abbreviate them using the initial letter of each parent's surname. Some women may argue that not all men are the same. To this, I say, 'What I am doing today is a testament to my husband's support and inspiration.' Therefore, I firmly assert that behind every successful woman, there stands an equally dynamic and supportive man. Women should not be treated as if they are less spirited or less dynamic."

At this point, everyone present requested Mr. Agarwal to share a few words. He said, "I would like to emphasize that women possess the power to guide men in various ways. My daughters have shown love, care, and trust in their relationships with their spouses. If we perceive husbands and wives as two halves of the same soul, working together to achieve greatness, they can unlock their inner potential. Love and trust thrive when egos are kept in check, and unrealistic desires are set aside.

Ride wrote this book. So, she ended with-----

Flying is not feasible without the pilot,
Family is not possible with likeminded couples.

About the Author

Yashodhara P

Yashodhara P (Jashodhara Purkayastha) started her writing career in 90's. Her debut book "Shaswat(106) poems" and Ease (English Grammar book for X &XII) was published from Create Space. She did not stop after that. Today, she has written 26 books. Four books are translated in Gujarati, Spanish, German and French.

Her book "Where Love Begins Vibhavari" was awarded the best fiction by editor of Lift magazine. She was nominated (0nly3 women were selected out of 25) by Atharva foundation of Mumbai in "Able and independent women "category. Yashodhara has received the Author of the year 2023

www.ingramcontent.com/pod-product-compliance
Lightning Source LLC
LaVergne TN
LVHW041539070526
838199LV00046B/1747